ARAMIS, FORMER MUSKETEER AND NOW BISHOP OF VANNES, HAD COME TO CONFESS A MYSTERIOUS PRISONER KNOWN ONLY AS MARCHIALI. BAISEMEAUX, GOVERNOR OF THE BASTILLE, ACCOMPANIED ARAMIS TO THE CELL.

WHEN THEY REACHED THE DOOR . . .

THE RULES DO NOT ALLOW THE GOVERNOR TO HEAR THE PRISONER'S CONFESSION.

A MOMENT LATER, ARAMIS WAS ALONE WITH THE PRISONER OF THE BASTILLE.

EVERY PRISONER HAS COMMITTED SOME CRIME. WHAT CRIME, THEN, HAVE YOU COMMITTED?

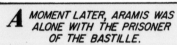

AS MY CONSCIENCE DOES NOT ACCUSE ME, I AVER I AM NOT A CRIMINAL.

WE ARE OFTEN CRIMINALS IN THE EYES OF THE GREAT, MERELY FOR KNOWING THAT A CRIME HAS BEEN COMMITTED.

YOU ARE HERE TO REVEAL IMPORTANT MATTERS TO ME. WHO ARE YOU?

DO YOU REMEMBER ONCE, IN THE VILLAGE WHERE YOU SPENT YOUR YOUTH, SEEING A CAVALIER, ACCOMPANIED BY A LADY IN BLACK?

I DO. AND I RECOGNISE YOU AS THAT CAVALIER.

THEN KNOW THIS ALSO. IF THE KING WERE TO LEARN THIS EVENING OF MY PRESENCE HERE, I WOULD TOMORROW SEE THE GLITTER OF THE EXECUTIONER'S AX. NOW, WHAT MORE DO YOU REMEMBER?

I REMEMBER WELL A WOMAN WHO CAME TO SEE ME EVERY MONTH. SHE, MY TUTOR, AND MY NURSE WERE THE ONLY PERSONS I EVER SPOKE TO.

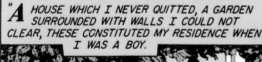

"*A* HOUSE WHICH I NEVER QUITTED, A GARDEN SURROUNDED WITH WALLS I COULD NOT CLEAR, THESE CONSTITUTED MY RESIDENCE WHEN I WAS A BOY.

"*I* LIVED AS CHILDREN DO, AS BIRDS, AS PLANTS AND THE SUN DO. THEN, ONE DAY, WHEN I HAD JUST TURNED MY FIFTEENTH YEAR . . .

"IT WAS VERY HOT AND I HAD FALLEN ASLEEP. I AWOKE TO HEAR MY TUTOR AND NURSE TALKING EXCITEDLY.

THE LETTER! THE LAST LETTER FROM THE QUEEN! IT'S IN THE WELL! THE WIND BLEW IT FROM MY HAND!

"I TREMBLED AT THESE WORDS. MY TUTOR IN CORRESPONDENCE WITH THE QUEEN!

CALM YOURSELF. 'T IS ALL THE SAME AS IF IT WERE BURNED, AS THE QUEEN BURNS ALL HER LETTERS EACH TIME SHE COMES HERE.

DOUBTLESS. BUT THIS LETTER CONTAINED INSTRUCTIONS. HOW CAN I FOLLOW THEM? I MUST GO DOWN THE WELL AND GET THE LETTER.

THEN THE LADY WHO COMES TO SEE ME EVERY MONTH IS THE QUEEN!

COME, WE WILL GET A LADDER LONG ENOUGH TO REACH THE WATER.

"WHEN THEY LEFT, I SPRANG THROUGH THE WINDOW AND RAN TO THE WELL.

"SOMETHING WHITE AND LUMINOUS GLISTENED IN THE GREEN RIPPLES.

"I LOWERED THE CORD AND BUCKET TO WITHIN THREE FEET OF THE WATER. THEN I SLID INTO THE ABYSS.

"I WAS SEIZED WITH GIDDINESS AND THE HAIR ROSE ON MY HEAD. BUT AT LAST I GAINED THE WATER AND SEIZED THE LETTER.

"I CONCEALED IT IN MY SHIRT AND REGAINED THE BRINK.

"THEN I RUSHED INTO THE SHRUBBERY TO READ MY PRIZE.

"*I READ ENOUGH TO LEARN THAT I MUST BE HIGH-BORN, SINCE THE QUEEN EARNESTLY COMMENDED ME TO THE CARE OF MY TUTOR. I HAD JUST TIME TO CONCEAL THE LETTER WHEN I WAS DISCOVERED.*"

PHILIPPE! YOU ARE WET THROUGH! WHAT HAS HAPPENED TO YOU?

"*THAT NIGHT, I WAS SEIZED WITH A VIOLENT CHILL AND AN ATTACK OF DELIRIUM, DURING WHICH I RELATED THE WHOLE ADVENTURE.*"

THE QUEEN... THE QUEEN... COMES TO SEE ME...

LOOK! UNDER HIS PILLOW! THE QUEEN'S LETTER!

POOR LAD, WHAT WILL HAPPEN TO HIM NOW?

DOUBTLESS, MY TUTOR, NOT DARING TO KEEP THE MATTER SECRET, WROTE ALL TO THE QUEEN. FOR SOON AFTER, I WAS BROUGHT HERE TO THE BASTILLE.

NOW I AM WEARY OF SPEAKING. IT IS YOUR TURN. CAN YOU TELL ME WHAT HAPPENED TO MY NURSE AND TUTOR?

THEY WERE MADE TO DISAPPEAR BY THE SUREST WAY POSSIBLE. BY POISON.

MY ENEMY MUST INDEED BE CRUEL TO MURDER THOSE INNOCENT PEOPLE.

IN YOUR FAMILY, MONSEIGNEUR, NECESSITY IS STERN. BUT ONE MORE QUESTION. IN YOUR HOUSE, WERE THERE EITHER LOOKING GLASSES OR MIRRORS?

WHAT IS THE MEANING OF THOSE TWO WORDS? I HAVE NO KNOWLEDGE OF THEM.

THEY ARE OBJECTS WHICH REFLECT ONE'S OWN IMAGE. TELL ME FURTHER, WERE YOU INSTRUCTED IN HISTORY?

VERY LITTLE.

IT WAS DONE BY DESIGN. JUST AS THEY DEPRIVED YOU OF MIRRORS, WHICH REFLECT THE PRESENT, SO THEY LEFT YOU IN IGNORANCE OF HISTORY, WHICH REFLECTS THE PAST.

LISTEN, THEN. I WILL TELL YOU WHAT HAS PASSED IN FRANCE FROM THE TIME OF YOUR BIRTH.

"*O*N THE FIFTH OF SEPTEMBER, 1638, ANNE OF AUSTRIA, WIFE OF LOUIS XIII, GAVE BIRTH TO A SON.

"*B*UT WHILE THE COURT AND KING WERE REJOICING OVER THE EVENT, THE QUEEN, ALONE IN HER ROOM EXCEPT FOR A MIDWIFE, GAVE BIRTH TO A SECOND SON.

"*T*HE MIDWIFE, WHO LATER BECAME YOUR NURSE, RAN AT ONCE AND WHISPERED THE NEWS TO THE KING.

"*T*HE KING'S JOY CHANGED TO TERROR.

TWIN SONS WILL MEAN DISCORD AND CIVIL WAR.

"*T*HE KING CONSULTED WITH HIS PRIME MINISTER.

TWIN SONS WILL SURELY BRING ABOUT A WAR OF SUCCESSION. THE SECOND SON MUST BE TAKEN AWAY WHERE NONE SHALL KNOW OF HIS EXISTENCE.

IT SHALL BE DONE. MY DYNASTY MUST BE PRESERVED.

"*A*ND SO, ONE NIGHT SOON AFTER, THE SECOND SON WAS SPIRITED AWAY FROM THE PALACE."

SO COMPLETELY DID THAT SECOND SON DISAPPEAR THAT NOT A SOUL IN FRANCE, SAVE HIS MOTHER, IS AWARE OF HIS EXISTENCE.

HIS MOTHER... HIS MOTHER, WHO HAS CAST HIM OFF.

HAVE YOU A PORTRAIT OF THE KING, LOUIS XIV, WHO AT THIS MOMENT REIGNS UPON THE THRONE?

HERE.

AND NOW, HERE IS A MIRROR.

WHICH OF THE TWO IS KING?

THE KING IS HE WHO IS ON THE THRONE, NOT HE WHO IS IN PRISON. YOU SEE HOW POWERLESS I AM.

I WILL GIVE YOU POWER. IF YOU DESIRE IT, I SHALL PLACE YOU UPON THE THRONE OF FRANCE.

TEMPT ME NOT, MONSIEUR.

BE NOT WEAK, MONSEIGNEUR.

HOW CAN YOU RESTORE ME TO THE RANK AND POWER WHICH MY MOTHER AND MY BROTHER HAVE DEPRIVED ME OF?

IT SHALL BE DONE.

AND WHAT WILL HAPPEN TO MY BROTHER?

A CRIME WAS COMMITTED AGAINST YOU IN RENDERING THOSE DIFFERENT IN FORTUNE WHO NATURE CREATED THE SAME IN THE WOMB. THE PUNISHMENT SHOULD RESTORE THE BALANCE.

BY WHICH YOU MEAN...

THAT WHEN I PUT YOU ON YOUR BROTHER'S THRONE, HE SHALL TAKE YOUR PLACE IN PRISON.

NOW, ADIEU, MONSEIGNEUR, UNTIL I COME TO FETCH YOU FROM THESE GLOOMY WALLS.

A MOMENT LATER, ARAMIS LEFT THE CELL AND REJOINED THE GOVERNOR OF THE BASTILLE.

WHAT A LONG CONFESSION! WHO WOULD BELIEVE THAT A RECLUSE HAD SINS SO LONG TO TELL OF!

A FEW DAYS LATER, ARAMIS CALLED ON MONSIEUR FOUQUET, FRANCE'S SUPERINTENDENT OF FINANCES.

AH, MY FRIEND, IS ALL IN READINESS FOR THE FESTIVAL YOU ARE TO GIVE IN HONOUR OF THE KING? EVERYONE TALKS OF HOW SPLENDID IT IS TO BE.

THE FESTIVAL IS APPROACHING. MONEY IS DEPARTING.

HAVE I NOT TOLD YOU THAT MONEY IS MY WORRY?

YES, YOU PROMISED ME MILLIONS.

YOU SHALL HAVE THEM -- THE DAY AFTER THE KING COMES TO YOUR CHATEAU AT VAUX FOR THE FESTIVAL.

AND NOW I WOULD LIKE A LETTER FROM YOU. I WISH TO HAVE A *LETTRE DE CACHET.*

LETTRE DE CACHET! DO YOU WISH TO PUT SOMEBODY IN THE BASTILLE?

ON THE CONTRARY, I WISH TO LET SOMEONE OUT.

WHO?

A POOR LAD NAMED SELDON, WHO HAS BEEN BASTILLED THESE TEN YEARS FOR TWO LATIN VERSES HE WROTE.

WHAT! YOU KNEW OF THIS INJUSTICE AND YOU NEVER TOLD ME?

'T WAS ONLY YESTERDAY HIS MOTHER APPLIED TO ME. POOR WOMAN, SHE LIVES IN DEEPEST POVERTY.

FOUQUET QUICKLY WROTE THE LETTER. THEN HE TOOK 10,000 FRANCS FROM HIS DESK.

SET THE SON AT LIBERTY AND GIVE THIS TO THE MOTHER. BUT DO NOT TELL HER THAT . . .

THAT WHAT, MONSEIGNEUR?

THAT SHE IS NOW 10,000 FRANCS RICHER THAN I. SHE WOULD SAY I AM INDEED A POOR SUPERINTENDENT OF FINANCES.

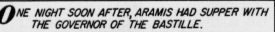

ONE NIGHT SOON AFTER, ARAMIS HAD SUPPER WITH THE GOVERNOR OF THE BASTILLE.

TO SEE YOU BOOTED AS A CAVALIER REMINDS ME OF PAST DAYS.

IT SHOULD. YOU WERE A MUSKETEER WITH US--WITH ATHOS AND PORTHOS AND D'ARTAGNAN. MORE WINE, BAISEMEAUX. LET US CELEBRATE THE OLD DAYS.

AN HOUR LATER, A CLATTER WAS HEARD IN THE COURTYARD. A COURIER HAD ARRIVED WITH A MESSAGE FOR THE GOVERNOR.

LET HIM GO TO THE DEVIL. I AM AT SUPPER.

TAKE CARE, FRIEND. THE MESSAGE MAY BE IMPORTANT.

BAISEMEAUX HAD THE MESSAGE BROUGHT UP.

AN ORDER OF RELEASE! THEY SEIZE A MAN, KEEP HIM FOR YEARS, THEN, WITHOUT WARNING, SAY, "RELEASE HIM AT ONCE." BAH! LET HIM WAIT UNTIL MORNING.

BOOTED THOUGH I BE, I AM A PRIEST. I ENTREAT YOU TO ABRIDGE THIS POOR MAN'S SUFFERING AT ONCE. GOD WILL REPAY YOU IN PARADISE.

IN THE MIDDLE OF OUR SUPPER? OH, VERY WELL, THEN, IF YOU WISH IT.

AS THE GOVERNOR CALLED FOR HIS MEN, ARAMIS CHANGED THE ORDER FOR ANOTHER.

THEN . . .

I WILL HAVE THE MAJOR GO AND OPEN THE CELL OF MONSIEUR SELDON.

YOU MEAN TO SAY *MARCHIALI.*

MARCHIALI? NO, NO--SELDON*!*

I SAW *SELDON* IN LETTERS LARGE AS THAT.

AND I READ *MARCHIALI* IN CHARACTERS AS LARGE AS THIS.

LOOK.

YES, 'T IS PLAINLY WRITTEN --MARCHIALI. THE MAN I HAVE ORDERS TO WATCH MOST CAREFULLY. I DO NOT UNDERSTAND IT.

BAISEMEAUX BECAME VERY SUSPICIOUS.

MARCHIALI IS THE VERY PRISONER WHOM A CERTAIN PRIEST OF THE JESUITS CAME TO VISIT THE OTHER NIGHT IN SO SECRET A MANNER.

WITH *US*, MONSIEUR, FOR YOU, TOO, ARE A MEMBER OF THE ORDER, IT IS GOOD THAT THE MAN OF TODAY FORGET THE MAN OF YESTERDAY.

IF A SUPERIOR OFFICER OF THE JESUITS GIVES YOU ORDERS, YOU WILL OBEY?

NEVER DOUBT IT, MONSEIGNEUR.

ARAMIS TOOK A PEN AND WROTE . . .

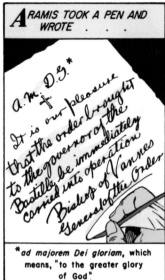

A. M. D. G.*

It is our pleasure that the order brought to the governor of the Bastille be immediately carried into operation

Bishop of Vannes
General of the Order

*ad majorem Dei gloriam, which means, "to the greater glory of God".

BAISEMEAUX WAS ASTONISHED.

YOU ARE GENERAL OF THE ORDER! TO THINK THAT I HAVE DARED TO TREAT YOU AS AN EQUAL!

SAY NOTHING OF IT, OLD COMRADE. TO YOU I GIVE MY PROTECTION AND FRIENDSHIP. TO ME YOU GIVE YOUR OBEDIENCE.

HAVE YOUR MEN BRING THE PRISONER MARCHIALI HERE.

A SHORT TIME LATER, THE DUNGEON RENDERED UP ITS PREY.

YOU WILL SWEAR NEVER TO REVEAL ANYTHING YOU HAVE SEEN OR HEARD IN THE BASTILLE.

PHILIPPE KISSED A CRUCIFIX, IN TOKEN OF HIS WORD.

NOW THAT YOU ARE FREE, WHITHER DO YOU INTEND GOING?

THEN ARAMIS STEPPED OUT OF THE SHADOWS.

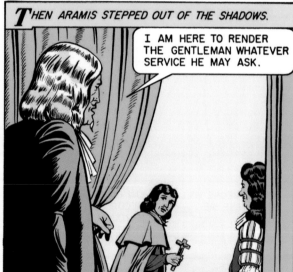

I AM HERE TO RENDER THE GENTLEMAN WHATEVER SERVICE HE MAY ASK.

SOON PHILIPPE AND ARAMIS ENTERED A CARRIAGE WHICH HAD BEEN KEPT IN READINESS. A FEW MINUTES LATER--NO MORE WALLS ON EITHER SIDE; LIBERTY EVERYWHERE, HEAVEN EVERYWHERE.

WHEN THEY HAD RIDDEN A SAFE DISTANCE, ARAMIS STOPPED THE CARRIAGE.

NOW WE CAN CONVERSE. MONSEIGNEUR, PROVIDENCE HAS GIVEN YOU THE FEATURES OF YOUR BROTHER. THIS VERY CAUSE OF YOUR IMPRISONMENT WILL NOW LEAD TO YOUR TRIUMPH.

THE DAY AFTER TOMORROW, YOU WILL SIT UPON THE THRONE, AND YOUR BROTHER WILL BE IN THE DUNGEON.

BUT SOMEONE WILL RECOGNISE ME.

HOW CAN ANYONE RECOGNISE YOU IF YOU ACT IN THE MANNER OF THE KING?

THE IMPRISONED KING WILL SPEAK.

TO WHOM? TO THE WALLS?

THERE IS YET ANOTHER OBSTACLE-- MY CONSCIENCE.

IT IS USELESS TO FLASH BRIGHT VISIONS BEFORE THE EYES OF ONE WHO LOVES DARKNESS. DO YOU WISH A MORE HUMBLE LIFE?

I KNOW OF A PLACE OF WHICH NO ONE IN FRANCE SUSPECTS THE EXISTENCE. THE SUN THERE IS SOFT, THE SOIL RICH, THE GAME PLENTIFUL.

YOU CAN GO THERE AND LIVE IN SAFETY, PEACE AND COMFORT. OR YOU CAN TAKE THE THRONE AND RISK DEATH. WHICH WILL YOU ACCEPT?

BEFORE I ANSWER, LET ME WALK ON THE GROUND AND CONSULT THAT STILL VOICE WITHIN ME WHICH HEAVEN SENDS US ALL.

WHEN PHILIPPE RETURNED TO THE CARRIAGE . . .

LET US GO WHERE THE CROWN OF FRANCE IS TO BE FOUND!

PROVIDENCE HAS SPOKEN. NOW LET US RESUME OUR CONVERSATION. HAVE YOU READ THE NOTES I HAD SMUGGLED TO YOU TO ACQUAINT YOU WITH YOUR COURT?

I KNOW THEM BY HEART.

"MY MOTHER, ANNE OF AUSTRIA, ALL HER SORROWS, HER PAINFUL MALADY. OH, I KNOW HER.

"COLBERT, MY MINISTER, IS UGLY AND DARK-BROWED. HE IS THE MORTAL ENEMY OF MONSIEUR FOUQUET.

"D'ARTAGNAN IS THE CAPTAIN OF MY MUSKETEERS. TO THIS BRAVE MAN THE CROWN OF FRANCE OWES SO MUCH IT OWES EVERYTHING. AND PORTHOS, THE HERCULES OF FRANCE. I SEE HIM, TOO, IN MY MIND'S EYE."

D'ARTAGNAN AND PORTHOS. YOUR FRIENDS, MONSIEUR.

YES, I CAN WELL SAY, "MY FRIENDS."

WHAT OF MONSIEUR FOUQUET? WHAT DO YOU WISH ME TO DO FOR HIM?

WHEN YOU SHALL HAVE PAID HIS DEBTS AND RESTORED THE COUNTRY'S FINANCES TO A SOUND CONDITION, WE SHALL RETIRE HIM TO HIS PLEASURES.

AND FOR YOURSELF?

FIRST, I WILL BE MADE A CARDINAL AND PRIME MINISTER OF FRANCE. THEN, SINCE I SHALL HAVE GIVEN YOU THE THRONE OF FRANCE, YOU WILL CONFER ON ME THE THRONE OF ST. PETER.

I WILL DO ALL THAT YOU DIRECT.

PHILIPPE AND ARAMIS RESUMED THEIR PLACES IN THE CARRIAGE. THEY SPED TOWARD VAUX, WHERE KING LOUIS XIV WOULD COME TO ATTEND FOUQUET'S FESTIVAL IN HIS HONOR.

THE NEXT DAY, AT VAUX, ARAMIS AND FOUQUET AWAITED THE ARRIVAL OF LOUIS XIV.

THE KING WILL SOON BE HERE. YOU CAN SEE HIS PROCESSION IN THE DISTANCE.

HE CARES FOR ME BUT LITTLE. BUT AS MY GUEST, HE IS MORE SACRED THAN EVER TO ME.

ARE YOU COMFORTABLE, MY FRIEND? WHAT APARTMENT HAVE YOU CHOSEN FOR YOUR LODGINGS?

THE BLUE ROOM ON THE SECOND STORY.

THE ROOM DIRECTLY OVER THE KING'S? WHAT AN IDEA, TO CONDEMN YOURSELF TO A ROOM WHERE YOU CANNOT STIR FOR FEAR OF DISTURBING HIS MAJESTY.

DO NOT FEAR. DURING THE NIGHT, I SLEEP OR READ IN MY BED.

AND YOUR SERVANTS?

I HAVE ONLY ONE PERSON WITH ME. ADIEU, MONSEIGNEUR. I SHALL SEE YOU LATER.

THAT NIGHT, A SPLENDID BANQUET WAS HELD FOR THE ROYAL GUESTS.

I AM HUMILIATED! FOUQUET HAS TREASURES UNKNOWN TO MY PALACE.

AFTER THE FEAST, THE KING WENT TO HIS ROOM.

TELL MONSIEUR COLBERT I WISH TO SEE HIM.

MEANWHILE, IN THE ROOM ABOVE, ARAMIS HAD A VISITOR.

WELCOME, D'ARTAGNAN! PORTHOS WOULD WELCOME YOU, TOO. BUT HE HAS DINED WELL AND YOU REMEMBER HOW SOUNDLY HE SLEEPS.

ARAMIS, DO YOU REMEMBER HOW YOU USED TO HAVE FAITH IN MY INSTINCTIVE FEELINGS? WELL, AN INSTINCT TELLS ME YOU ARE PLOTTING SOMETHING.

WHAT NONSENSE!

NO--A VOICE WHICH HAS NEVER YET DECEIVED ME SPEAKS WITHIN ME. IT IS THE KING YOU ARE CONSPIRING AGAINST.

YOU ARE MAD. BESIDES, DO YOU NOT HAVE YOUR GUARDS AND MUSKETEERS HERE TO PROTECT HIM?

TRUE. BUT GRANT ME, ARAMIS, THE WORD OF A TRUE FRIEND. SAY THERE IS NO PLOT.

IF I THINK OF HARMING THE SON OF ANNE OF AUSTRIA, THE TRUE KING OF THIS REALM, MAY HEAVEN'S LIGHTNING BLAST ME WHERE I STAND!

VERY WELL. I BELIEVE YOU.

*T*HEN D'ARTAGNAN WOKE PORTHOS.

COME, I WILL TAKE YOU TO YOUR ROOM.

GOOD NIGHT, MY FRIENDS. IN TEN MINUTES, I SHALL BE FAST ASLEEP.

*B*UT AS SOON AS ARAMIS WAS ALONE, PHILIPPE APPEARED FROM BEHIND A SLIDING PANEL.

MONSIEUR D'ARTAGNAN IS EXTREMELY SUSPICIOUS. HE SEEMS VERY DEVOTED TO THE KING.

HE IS AS FAITHFUL AS A DOG. BUT HE BITES SOMETIMES.

WHAT ARE WE TO DO NOW?

YOU WILL OBSERVE THE CEREMONY OF THE KING'S RETIRING, SO AS TO LEARN HOW IT IS PERFORMED.

*H*E PUSHED ASIDE A PORTION OF THE FLOORING.

CAN YOU SEE?

YES. MONSIEUR COLBERT IS WITH THE KING.

WHAT! IT BODES ILL FOR MONSIEUR FOUQUET. LET ME SEE.

COLBERT, FOUQUET HAS ECLIPSED ME. HIS TABLE GROANS WITH DELIGHTS THAT HAVE NEVER GRACED MY OWN. WHERE DOES HE GET HIS WEALTH?

FROM YOUR OWN POCKET, SIRE. I HAVE DISCOVERED A DEFICIT IN FOUQUET'S PUBLIC ACCOUNTS. IT IS YOUR MONEY HE SPENDS ON THIS DISPLAY.

COLBERT IS A LIAR AND A SCOUNDREL!

NOW YOU SEE THE SOURCE OF FOUQUET'S GREAT WEALTH, SIRE.

IF THIS CAN BE PROVED...

IT IS SO, ALREADY.

MISERABLE WRETCH! FAITHLESS SERVANT! FOUQUET'S FESTIVAL SHALL TURN TO ASHES FOR THIS.

GO NOW, AND SEND ME THE CAPTAIN OF THE MUSKETEERS.

FIVE MINUTES LATER, D'ARTAGNAN STOOD BEFORE LOUIS XIV.

PLACE MONSIEUR FOUQUET UNDER ARREST!

WHAT? ARREST HIM IN HIS OWN HOUSE? WHILE YOU ARE UNDER HIS ROOF-- HIS GUEST?

THE KING IS MASTER, WHEREVER HE MAY BE!

THE KING IS MASTER IN A MAN'S HOUSE ONLY WHEN HE HAS DRIVEN THE OWNER OUT OF IT. THINK, SIRE, DO NOT BRING SHAME UPON YOUR HEAD.

I HATE HIM! TOMORROW HE SHALL FALL SO LOW THAT EVERYONE WILL KNOW I AM INDEED GREATER THAN HE. GO! KEEP HIM UNDER YOUR GUARD!

IT IS YOUR WISH, AND IT SHALL BE DONE. BUT, SIRE! TO ARREST IN HIS OWN HOUSE A MAN WHO IS RUINING HIMSELF TO PLEASE YOU!

GUARD MONSIEUR FOUQUET TONIGHT AND RETURN IN THE MORNING FOR FURTHER ORDERS. NOW LEAVE ME!

WHEN D'ARTAGNAN HAD GONE, THE KING THREW HIMSELF ON HIS BED.

WHILE ABOVE HIS HEAD...

NOW THE KING WILL SLEEP. HAVING RETIRED AS A CROWNED SOVEREIGN, HE WILL AWAKEN IN CAPTIVITY.

MY BROTHER WILL DISAPPEAR SO SIMPLY?

A SECRET CONTRIVANCE WHICH YIELDS TO THE PRESSURE OF A FINGER WILL LOWER THE BED TO AN UNDERGROUND PASSAGEWAY. IT WILL RETURN EMPTY.

THEN THE SAME CONTRIVANCE WILL LOWER A PORTION OF THIS FLOOR, AND YOU WILL BE IN THE KING'S PLACE. FROM THAT MOMENT, YOU ALONE WILL RULE.

I GO NOW TO ALERT MY FAITHFUL PORTHOS, WHO WILL HELP ME RECEIVE THE DEPOSED KING.

BELOW, EXHAUSTED BY HIS FURY, THE KING BEGAN TO FALL ASLEEP. AS HIS EYES CLOSED, HE FANCIED A FACE GAZING DOWN AT HIM IN PROFOUND PITY--A FACE AS MUCH HIS OWN AS THOUGH IT WERE REFLECTED IN A MIRROR.

A GENTLE, EASY MOVEMENT, AS REGULAR AS THAT BY WHICH A VESSEL PLUNGES BENEATH THE WAVES, SUCCEEDED TO THE IMMOBILITY OF THE BED.

THE CEILING SEEMED TO BE GRADUALLY GETTING FURTHER AND FURTHER AWAY.

THE KING, HALF-AWAKENED, THOUGHT HIMSELF UNDER THE INFLUENCE OF A TERRIBLE DREAM. SOMETHING COLD AND GLOOMY SEEMED TO INFECT THE AIR.

AFTER A MINUTE WHICH SEEMED AN AGE TO THE KING, THE BED REACHED A LEVEL OF AIR BLACK AND STILL AS DEATH. THEN IT STOPPED.

IT IS TIME TO WAKEN FROM THIS MAD DREAM. COME, LET ME WAKE UP.

THEN . . . .

WHAT IS THE MEANING OF THIS JEST?

IT IS NO JEST. WE ARE YOUR MASTERS, NOW. BE GOOD ENOUGH TO FOLLOW US.

WHAT DO YOU INTEND TO DO WITH THE KING OF FRANCE?

YOU DESERVE TO BE BROKEN ON THE WHEEL FOR CALLING YOURSELF THAT.

THE KING WAS LED TO A CARRIAGE THAT WAITED AT THE END OF THE PASSAGEWAY.

IT SEEMS I HAVE FALLEN INTO THE HANDS OF ASSASSINS.

THE CARRIAGE DROVE TO THE BASTILLE, WHERE ARAMIS ROUSED THE GOVERNOR.

WHAT IS THE MATTER NOW? WHOM HAVE YOU BROUGHT ME?

LET US GO TO YOUR ROOM. I WILL EXPLAIN THERE.

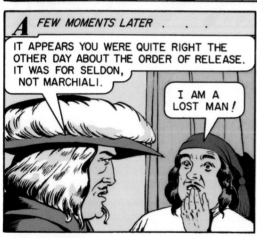

A FEW MOMENTS LATER . . .

IT APPEARS YOU WERE QUITE RIGHT THE OTHER DAY ABOUT THE ORDER OF RELEASE. IT WAS FOR SELDON, NOT MARCHIALI.

I AM A LOST MAN!

FAR FROM IT. SINCE I HAVE MARCHIALI BACK, IT IS JUST THE SAME AS IF HE NEVER LEFT.

BUT WHY DID YOU BRING HIM BACK?

FROM YOU, MY FRIEND, I HAVE NO SECRETS. YOU HAVE NO DOUBT NOTED THE RESEMBLANCE BETWEEN THAT FELLOW AND THE KING?

YES.

WELL, THE WRETCH MADE USE OF HIS LIBERTY BY PRETENDING TO BE THE KING HIMSELF! THE KING IS FURIOUS!

LET US RETURN THIS MADMAN TO HIS CELL AT ONCE!

THEY RETURNED TO THE COURTYARD.

AH! SO YOU ARE BACK, YOU MISERABLE WRETCH.

A MOMENT LATER, THE KING, TOO STUNNED TO SPEAK, WAS LED TO PHILIPPE'S CELL.

IN WITH YOU!

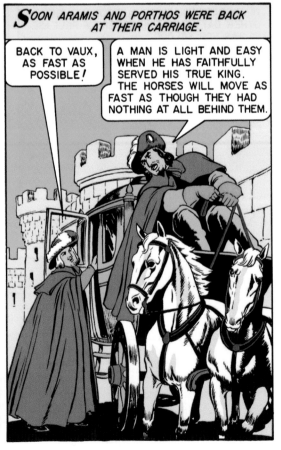

SOON ARAMIS AND PORTHOS WERE BACK AT THEIR CARRIAGE.

BACK TO VAUX, AS FAST AS POSSIBLE!

A MAN IS LIGHT AND EASY WHEN HE HAS FAITHFULLY SERVED HIS TRUE KING. THE HORSES WILL MOVE AS FAST AS THOUGH THEY HAD NOTHING AT ALL BEHIND THEM.

THE KING, ALONE IN HIS CELL, WAS STILL IN A STUPOR.

AM I DEAD? IS THIS WHAT IS TERMED HELL?

THEN HE LOOKED DOWN.

A CRY ESCAPED HIM, AND HE RETURNED TO HIS SENSES.

A PRISONER! I -- I, A PRISONER!

THERE IS A GOVERNOR IN THIS PLACE. I WILL SUMMON HIM TO ME.

WHERE IS THE GOVERNOR? I WANT TO SPEAK TO THE GOVERNOR!

BUT NO VOICE REPLIED TO HIS.

*H*E BROKE A CHAIR AND USED THE LEG TO STRIKE THE DOOR.

OPEN! OPEN IN THE KING'S NAME!

*W*HEN NO ONE ANSWERED, HE LEAPED FROM THE TABLE TO THE WINDOW AND BROKE A PANE OF GLASS.

THE GOVERNOR! I WANT TO SEE THE GOVERNOR!

*I*N TIME, A JAILER CAME TO BRING HIM FOOD.

YOU HAVE BROKEN YOUR CHAIR. WHY, YOU MUST HAVE GONE QUITE MAD.

MONSIEUR, ASK THE GOVERNOR TO COME TO ME.

COME, MY BOY. YOU HAVE BROKEN YOUR CHAIR AND MADE A GREAT DISTURBANCE. PROMISE ME NOT TO BEGIN OVER AGAIN, AND I WILL NOT SAY A WORD TO THE GOVERNOR.

I WISH TO SEE THE GOVERNOR!

AH, YOUR EYES ARE BECOMING WILD. I SHALL HAVE TO TAKE AWAY YOUR KNIFE.

THE JAILER LEFT. NOW THE KING'S RAGE AND FRENZY KNEW NO BOUNDS.

HE TORE AT THE DOOR WITH HIS NAILS AND UTTERED WILD AND FEARFUL CRIES.

TWO HOURS AFTERWARD, LOUIS XIV COULD NOT BE RECOGNISED AS A KING—A GENTLEMAN—A HUMAN BEING.

MEANWHILE, AT VAUX, PHILIPPE HAD DESCENDED INTO THE ROYAL CHAMBER AND LAY, SLEEPLESS, IN LOUIS' BED.

I AM NOW FACE TO FACE WITH MY DESTINY.

TOWARD MORNING, A SHADOW GLIDED INTO THE ROOM.

WELL, MONSIEUR?

ALL IS DONE, SIRE.

HE IS IN YOUR CELL. THE GOVERNOR OF THE BASTILLE SUSPECTS NOTHING.

AT THAT MOMENT, DAWN CAME. A MINUTE LATER, THERE WAS A KNOCK ON THE DOOR.

THAT MUST BE D'ARTAGNAN TO REQUEST FURTHER ORDERS ON THE DISPOSITION OF MONSIEUR FOUQUET. NOW WE BEGIN THE ATTACK.

TO START WITH D'ARTAGNAN WOULD BE MADNESS. THE KEENEST SCENT IN FRANCE WOULD BE SURE TO DETECT SOMETHING HAS TAKEN PLACE IN THIS ROOM. I WILL SEND HIM AWAY.

D'ARTAGNAN WAS ASTOUNDED WHEN THE DOOR OPENED.

ARAMIS! YOU HERE?

THE KING DOES NOT WISH TO BE DISTURBED. HOWEVER, HE INSTRUCTS YOU TO SET MONSIEUR FOUQUET AT LIBERTY. I SHALL GO WITH YOU TO WITNESS HIS DELIGHT.

BUT HOW HAVE YOU BECOME SO MUCH A FAVOURITE OF THE KING THAT YOU CAN TRANSMIT ORDERS IN HIS NAME? YOU HAVE NEVER SPOKEN TO HIM MORE THAN TWICE IN YOUR LIFE.

THE FACT IS, I HAVE SPOKEN TO HIM MORE THAN A HUNDRED TIMES, ONLY WE HAVE KEPT IT SECRET. SO NOW YOU UNDERSTAND EVERYTHING.

AH, OF COURSE. NOW I UNDERSTAND.

NO, I DO NOT UNDERSTAND--YET.

IN FOUQUET'S ROOM . . .

SO, CAPTAIN, YOU HAVE BROUGHT THE BISHOP OF VANNES TO SEE YOUR PRISONER.

AND SOMETHING BETTER STILL-- LIBERTY. YOU ARE FREE, BY HIS MAJESTY'S ORDER.

THEN D'ARTAGNAN LEFT.

I DO NOT UNDERSTAND. WHAT DOES THIS MEAN?

THE KING BELIEVES YOU TO BE GUILTY OF STEALING PUBLIC FUNDS. HE IS ALSO ENVIOUS OF THE MAGNITUDE OF THE FESTIVAL YOU ARE GIVING IN HIS HONOUR. HE PROCLAIMS YOU A TRAITOR AND A THIEF.

THEN I DO NOT SEE -- WHY AM I PARDONED?

DO YOU REALLY THINK IT LIKELY THE KING WOULD PARDON YOU?

YOU ALARM ME. YOU ARE CONCEALING SOMETHING. WHAT IS THERE BETWEEN YOU AND THE KING?

A SECRET. ONE OF A NATURE TO CHANGE THE INTERESTS OF THE KING OF FRANCE.

THEN ARAMIS TOLD FOUQUET EVERYTHING.

GREAT GOD! THE KING DETHRONED? IMPRISONED? AND SUCH A CRIME HAS BEEN COMMITTED UNDER MY ROOF?

YOU DARED DO THIS -- WHILE THE KING WAS MY GUEST -- IN THE PROTECTION OF MY HOUSE?

YOUR HOUSE, YES. FOR MONSIEUR COLBERT CANNOT HAVE THE KING ROB YOU OF IT NOW.

YOU DARED TO COMMIT THIS CRIME HERE? THIS ABOMINABLE CRIME WHICH DISHONOURS MY NAME FOREVER!

CRIME? YOU ARE NOT IN YOUR SENSES, MONSEIGNEUR. THE KING'S IMPRISONMENT SAVES YOUR LIFE!

YOU MAY HAVE BEEN ACTING ON MY BEHALF, BUT I WILL NOT ACCEPT YOUR SERVICES. YOU WILL LEAVE MY HOUSE. I GIVE YOU FOUR HOURS TO PUT YOURSELF OUT OF THE KING'S REACH.

GO AT ONCE--TO SAVE YOUR LIFE. I GO TO MY SOVEREIGN TO SAVE MY HONOUR.

A RAMIS HURRIED TO PORTHOS' ROOM.

LOST! ALL IS LOST! SHALL I WARN PHILIPPE? TAKE HIM WITH ME? CIVIL WAR WOULD FOLLOW.

LET DESTINY BE FULFILLED. CONDEMNED WAS PHILIPPE, LET HIM REMAIN SO.

A FEW MINUTES LATER, D'ARTAGNAN WAS SURPRISED TO SEE ARAMIS AND PORTHOS RIDING OFF.

ADIEU, OLD FRIEND!

ON ANY OTHER OCCASION, I SHOULD SAY THOSE TWO WERE MAKING THEIR ESCAPE. BUT LET ME ATTEND TO MY OWN AFFAIRS; THAT IS QUITE ENOUGH.

MEANWHILE, FOUQUET HAD RUSHED TO THE BASTILLE. WHEN HE ENTERED THE KING'S CELL . . .

HAVE YOU COME TO ASSASSINATE ME, MONSIEUR FOUQUET?

SIRE, DO YOU NOT RECOGNISE THE MOST FAITHFUL OF YOUR FRIENDS?

A FRIEND-- YOU?

I AM THE MOST RESPECTFUL OF YOUR SERVANTS.

WAS IT NOT YOU WHO HAD ME BROUGHT HERE?

YOU CANNOT BELIEVE ME TO BE GUILTY OF SUCH AN ACT.

AND FOUQUET TOLD THE KING EVERYTHING HE KNEW.

SO! IT WAS THE BISHOP OF VANNES WHO LED THIS PLOT. AND THIS IMPOSTOR, PHILIPPE! HE MUST DIE!

ROYAL BLOOD CANNOT BE SHED ON THE SCAFFOLD.

ROYAL BLOOD! YOU BELIEVE THAT RIDICULOUS STORY OF THE DOUBLE BIRTH?

I DOUBT IT NOT, SIRE. PHILIPPE OF FRANCE IS YOUR BROTHER. THERE MUST BE NO PUBLIC TRIAL. THE AUGUST NAME OF YOUR MOTHER MUST NOT BE TOUCHED BY SCANDAL.

COME. LET US RETURN TO VAUX AND SEE THIS PHILIPPE. BUT FIRST, I SHALL STOP AT THE LOUVRE AND CHANGE MY CLOTHES.

SOON, BAISEMEAUX, COMPLETELY BEWILDERED BY THESE STRANGE EVENTS, WAS WATCHING MARCHIALI ONCE AGAIN LEAVE THE BASTILLE.

FOUQUET HAD GIVEN HIM AN ORDER TO RELEASE THE PRISONER AND ON IT THE PRISONER HIMSELF HAD WRITTEN . . .

Seen and approved Louis XIV

ROYAL BLOOD CANNOT BE SHED ON THE SCAFFOLD.

ROYAL BLOOD! YOU BELIEVE THAT RIDICULOUS STORY OF THE DOUBLE BIRTH?

I DOUBT IT NOT, SIRE. PHILIPPE OF FRANCE IS YOUR BROTHER. THERE MUST BE NO PUBLIC TRIAL. THE AUGUST NAME OF YOUR MOTHER MUST NOT BE TOUCHED BY SCANDAL.

COME. LET US RETURN TO VAUX AND SEE THIS PHILIPPE. BUT FIRST, I SHALL STOP AT THE LOUVRE AND CHANGE MY CLOTHES.

SOON, BAISEMEAUX, COMPLETELY BEWILDERED BY THESE STRANGE EVENTS, WAS WATCHING MARCHIALI ONCE AGAIN LEAVE THE BASTILLE.

FOUQUET HAD GIVEN HIM AN ORDER TO RELEASE THE PRISONER AND ON IT THE PRISONER HIMSELF HAD WRITTEN . . .

Seen and approved Louis XIV

AT VAUX, PHILIPPE HAD BEGUN TO PLAY HIS PART, EXPECTING ARAMIS AT ANY MOMENT TO APPEAR AT HIS SIDE TO GIVE HIM COUNSEL.

WHEN PHILIPPE WAS DRESSED, SEVERAL MEMBERS OF THE COURT ENTERED. HE TREMBLED WHEN HE RECOGNISED HIS MOTHER.

THIS IS THE WOMAN WHO SACRIFICED HER CHILD FOR REASONS OF STATE.

BUT SHE IS SO NOBLE, SO RAVAGED BY HER ILLNESSES. I WILL TRY TO LOVE HER AS A SON SHOULD.

PHILIPPE DREADED MOST THE APPEARANCE OF LOUIS' WIFE. BUT . . .

THE QUEEN DESIRES YOU TO KNOW THAT SHE IS FATIGUED AND WILL KEEP TO HER BED THIS MORNING.

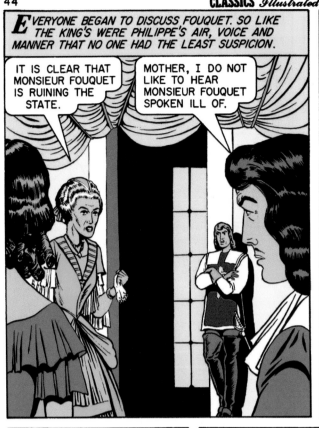

EVERYONE BEGAN TO DISCUSS FOUQUET. SO LIKE THE KING'S WERE PHILIPPE'S AIR, VOICE AND MANNER THAT NO ONE HAD THE LEAST SUSPICION.

IT IS CLEAR THAT MONSIEUR FOUQUET IS RUINING THE STATE.

MOTHER, I DO NOT LIKE TO HEAR MONSIEUR FOUQUET SPOKEN ILL OF.

NOR DO I LIKE UNNATURAL CRIMES, AND PLOTS TO KEEP THEM SECRET.

SECRET CRIMES! SIRE, YOU SPEAK CRUELLY TO YOUR MOTHER.

SO AGITATED WAS THE QUEEN AT HEARING THESE WORDS, THAT PHILIPPE HAD PITY ON HER. IN HIS HEART, HE FORGAVE HER FOR HIS YEARS OF SUFFERING.

DEAR MOTHER, I WISH ONLY THAT THERE BE PEACE BETWEEN YOU AND MY FRIENDS.

AS TIME PASSED, PHILIPPE BEGAN TO WONDER ABOUT THE ABSENCE OF ARAMIS.

D'ARTAGNAN, WHERE IS YOUR FRIEND, THE BISHOP OF VANNES? BRING HIM TO ME.

BUT SIRE, HE . . .

AT THAT MOMENT, A LOUD VOICE WAS HEARD.

IT IS THE VOICE OF MONSIEUR FOUQUET!

THE DOOR OPENED. THEN PHILIPPE SAW WHAT HE LITTLE THOUGHT TO SEE.

BY CHANCE, LOUIS HAD DRESSED HIMSELF IN THE SAME COSTUME THAT PHILIPPE WORE. EACH WAS TO THE OTHER AS A FORM REFLECTED IN A GLASS.

THEN LOUIS WENT UP TO THE QUEEN MOTHER.

MY MOTHER, DO YOU NOT ACKNOWLEDGE YOUR KING?

PHILIPPE ALSO STEPPED FORWARD.

MY MOTHER, DO YOU NOT ACKNOWLEDGE YOUR SON?

AT THIS, LOUIS TURNED TO D'ARTAGNAN.

LOOK US IN THE FACE AND SEE WHO IS KING. SAY WHICH OF US IS PALER, HE OR I!

D'ARTAGNAN WALKED DIRECTLY TO PHILIPPE.

MONSEIGNEUR, YOU ARE MY PRISONER.

ALEXANDRE DUMAS

WHEN Alexandre Dumas submitted his first play for criticism, he was asked, "Have you any other means of existence?" When he replied that he was a clerk, he was told, "Go back to your desk, young man, go back to your desk."

But Dumas did not follow this advice. He went on to become a very successful dramatist and author. As a result of his writings, he became so famous that the street in a small town outside of Paris where he was born in 1802, was renamed after him.

Life was not easy for Dumas when he was a child. His father, who was a general in Napoleon's army, died when Dumas was only four. Dumas and his mother were left with little more than the land they lived on. They had to struggle to get along and Dumas received very little education. When he grew older, he worked as a lawyer's messenger and later became a clerk in Paris.

Dumas had always been interested in the theater and while he was doing his clerking, he began writing plays. When the idea for the plot of a play came to him, he would recite the lines bit by bit to himself and his friends. When the play was finally clear and complete in his mind, he wrote it all down.

In 1828, the committee of the *Theatre Francais* accepted one of his plays, *Henri III*, for presentation. It was an immediate success. On the morning after the play opened, Dumas was seized by the editor of an illustrated paper and led to the studio of an artist who then and there made a drawing of him for the paper. Dumas' appearance soon became a very familiar one around Paris. He later wrote, "My success, if not the best deserved, was at any rate one of the most sensational of the time."

In 1839, Dumas met Auguste Maquet who was a student of history, a lecturer and a writer. Maquet became Dumas' collaborator on many books. He supplied the historical research and Dumas, with his boundless imagination, expanded the research into stories like *The Three Musketeers* and *The Count of Monte Cristo*.

Dumas got the idea for his novel, *The Count of Monte Cristo*, after taking a trip to the island of Elba. After the trip, he and a companion were on board their ship travelling to an island near Elba for hunting, when they saw in the distance a rock jutting out of the sea. When Dumas asked what it was, he was told that it was the island of Monte Cristo. The name caught Dumas' fancy. Although he never visited the island because it was under quarantine, he never forgot it.

Dumas became a very wealthy man through his writings. But he lived extravagantly, like a character out of his own books, and his activities led him into debt. His downfall began with the building of a magnificent house called Monte Cristo. The day the house was finished, Dumas invited 600 guests to see it.

The house had many guest rooms and when people came to visit, they usually stayed on and on, spending Dumas' money as fast as he earned it. Occasionally, some of the guests would try to make themselves useful in return for their keep. For one man, Dumas invented the duty of going every day to check what the thermometer registered and report it to him.

During all of this time, Dumas continued to write, with the aid of several collaborators, and he made much money. But high living and high spending wore him out. He was near poverty when he died in 1870, at the age of sixty-eight.